A Note to Grown-ups

One day, I watched my youngest child getting angry – and I decided to write
a poem about it, which has now been turned into this picture-book.
I wanted to explore the idea that anger takes over the whole world, because,
when you're very little, being angry is in part about wishing you were bigger.

By gently laughing at one of these big rages, I hope a child will see their
tantrum alongside that of the character in this book – and that,
even if anger can feel terrifyingly BIG, it doesn't usually last long!

For Emma, Elsie, Emile
and Joni. *M.R.*

For Elsie. *R.S.*

First published 2021 by Walker Books Ltd, 87 Vauxhall Walk, London SE11 5HJ

10 9 8 7 6 5 4 3 2 1

Text © 2021 Michael Rosen • Illustrations © 2021 Robert Starling

The right of Michael Rosen and Robert Starling to be identified as author and illustrator respectively of this work has
been asserted by them in accordance with the Copyright, Designs and Patents Act 1988

This work has been typeset in Futura T

Printed in China

British Library Cataloguing in Publication Data:
a catalogue record for this book is available from the British Library

ISBN 978-1-4063-9665-2

www.walker.co.uk

I AM ANGRY

Michael Rosen

ILLUSTRATED BY
Robert Starling

WALKER BOOKS
AND SUBSIDIARIES

LONDON • BOSTON • SYDNEY • AUCKLAND

Angry, angry, angry!

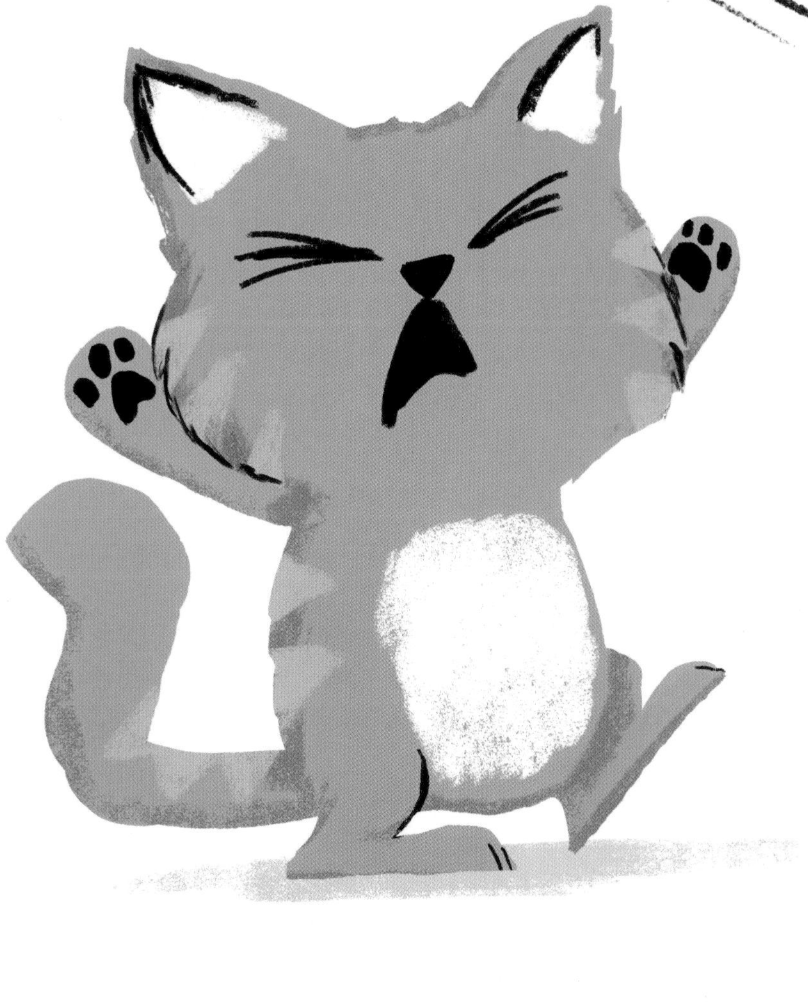

I'm so angry, I'll ...

up

jump   and

down,

roll on the ground,

make a **din,**

make you spin,

throw you in the bin!

I'll ...
knock down trees,
bully bees,

scare spiders,

scare tigers,

ROAR!

(MIAOW)

catch cockatoos,

confuse
kangaroos!

I'll ... bang all the bones, smash up stones,

silence birds ...

burst balloons,

squash the moon,

make

giants

run,

terrify the **sun**,

turn the sky red ...

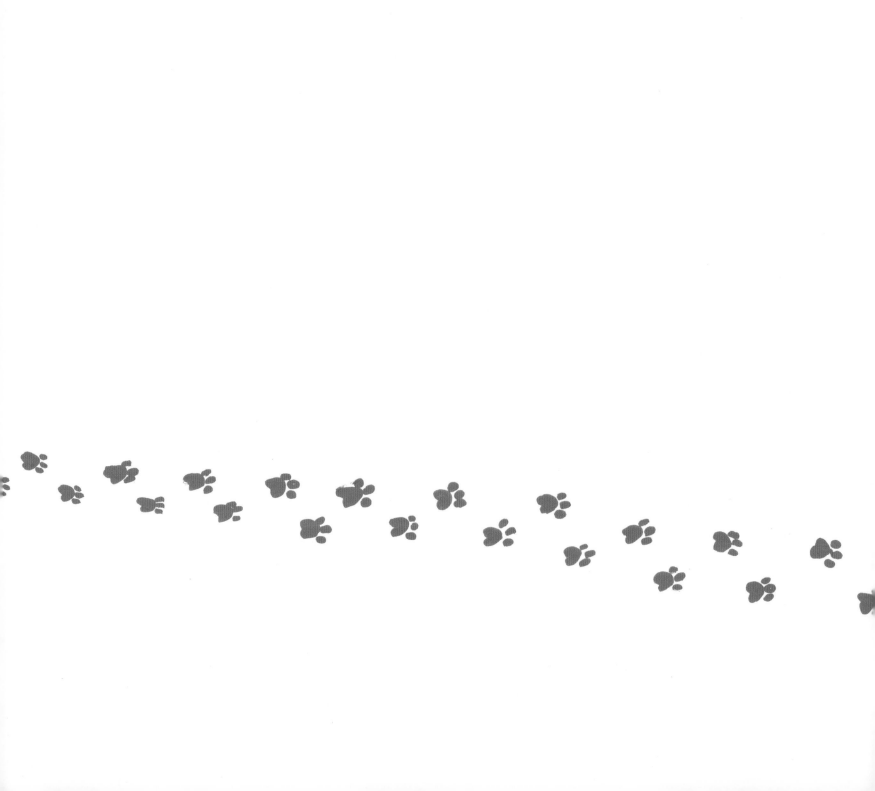

and go to bed.

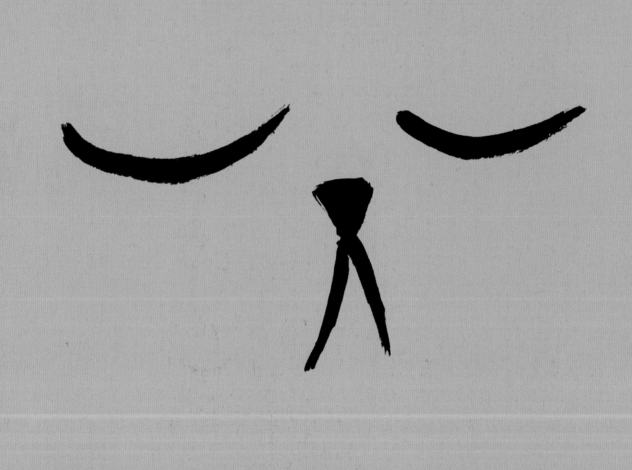